Michael

Story by Tony Bradman
Pictures by Tony Ross

Andersen Press · London

First published in Great Britain in 1990 by Andersen Press Ltd., 20 Vauxhall Bridge Road,
London SW1V 2SA.
This paperback edition first published in 1997 by Andersen Press Ltd.
Published in Australia by Random House Australia Pty., 20 Alfred Street, Milsons Point,
Sydney, NSW 2061. All rights reserved. Colour separated in Switzerland by Photolitho AG,
Offsetreproduktionen, Gossau, Zürich. Printed and bound in Italy by Grafiche AZ, Verona.

10   9   8   7   6   5   4   3   2   1

British Library Cataloguing in Publication Data available.

ISBN 0 86264 759 2

This book has been printed on acid-free paper

Michael was different.

His teachers said . . .

he was the worst boy in the school.

He was always late…

and he was a little scruffy.

He was often cheeky.

And he never did what he was told, either.

"That boy will come to no good," his teachers said.

But Michael didn't listen.

Michael didn't listen in the lessons, either.

He liked reading . . .

but not the sort of books they had in school.

He liked numbers . . .

but not the sort of sums they did in school.

He liked art . . .

but not the sort of drawing they did in school.

He liked science . . .

but not the sort of experiments they did in school.

"We give up!" said the teachers. "Come away children."

Michael didn't care. He knew what he was doing.

"It will never work," said the teachers.

All Michael said was, "Ten, nine, eight, seven, six...

five, four, three, two, one…"

Blast off! And the teachers said...

"We always knew that boy would go far."